Octavia   Enobarbus

Cleopatra's ladies in waiting

Antony's soldiers

"*I*t's a disgrace," said one of the soldiers to another. "Our general's behaving like a silly love-sick schoolboy, and it's all because of that woman. She's made a real fool of him! Doesn't he *care* what people are saying about him?"

It was the talk of the Egyptian court at Alexandria. General Mark Antony was one of the three most powerful men in the whole world. The great Julius Caesar had been the ruler of the mighty Roman Empire, and after he was murdered, Antony and two other generals, Octavius and Lepidus, had agreed to rule the Empire between them. Antony was a brave soldier who had won many battles and brought fame and glory to Rome. Everyone admired his courage and his troops loved him.

"Antony knows more about soldiering than Octavius and Lepidus put together," they used to say. "Everybody knows that. No wonder Octavius is a bit jealous of him."

But Antony had fallen in love with Cleopatra, the beautiful and mysterious queen of Egypt. It was as if she had put a spell on him. Instead of being in Rome, making important decisions, Antony preferred to stay in Alexandria at Cleopatra's court, feasting and getting drunk.

"Let the Empire take care of itself," he said, lying back on silk cushions after yet another great banquet. "This is the life, and this is where I belong!"

But the soldiers were horrified. There were even rumours that one night Antony had let Cleopatra dress him up in her robes, while she paraded about in his armour, carrying his great sword. He had gone too far!

Queen Cleopatra was as clever as she was beautiful, and she ruled her people wisely. But she had a terrible temper and everyone was a little afraid of her moods. She was happy one minute and sad the next. It was as if she was living her life like an actress on stage.

For no reason at all, she would suddenly command one of her servants, "Hey, you! Find Antony. If he's in a good mood, tell him I've been taken ill. If he looks sad, tell him I'm dancing and having a good time. And get back here quickly – I want to know how he looks when you tell him!"

But Antony knew better than to cross her. However much she teased and provoked him, he always forgave her in the end, although sometimes even his patience was exhausted.

"Be careful, madam," warned Cleopatra's ladies-in-waiting "One day you'll go too far. Don't push him."

"Nonsense," Cleopatra would say with a secret smile, "I know just how to handle him."

One day there was urgent news from Rome. Pompey, the son of one of Julius Caesar's old enemies, was gathering an army to rebel against the rulers of the Empire, and was growing more powerful by the day. This was a crisis, and Octavius needed Antony back in Rome.

Cleopatra, of course, threw one of her usual tantrums as soon as Antony got ready to leave. "Oh, go, then, leave me and go back to Rome – I see now how little I mean to you!" she wailed theatrically.

"Don't be silly, this is serious," Antony tried to reason with her. "I promise I'll soon be back."

In spite of Cleopatra's tears, Antony set off for Rome with Enobarbus, his loyal captain.

Octavius and Antony admired each other, but they had never really been friends. In fact, they didn't quite trust one another. Octavius was much younger than Antony and he was very ambitious. He was also a very serious young man. He had never had any time for Antony's foolish behaviour, and he was furious with him now for neglecting his duties.

"When I think what a great soldier he used to be," he fumed, "what an example to the troops! He was braver than any of them: he could stand the longest marches, the most harsh conditions. I could tell you things that would make your hair stand on end. And now look at him...

It's one thing behaving like this in peacetime, but the Empire is at stake here. What on earth can we do to bring him to his senses?"

Then one of his captains came up with a brilliant idea. "You have a sister, sir," he said to Octavius, "the lady Octavia. What if Antony married her? That would be a kind of peace treaty between the two of you. And if Antony were married to Octavia, he'd have to stay in Rome and behave properly. There would be no more gallivanting off to Egypt!"

Antony weighed up the proposal. Far away from Cleopatra, her hold on him was not so strong. To everybody's surprise, he agreed to the plan.

Soon, Antony and Octavia were married, and everyone was delighted, except for tough old Enobarbus, who had been with Antony for years. He knew his master too well. "He'll never be able to stay away from Egypt," he thought. "There's sure to be trouble ahead."

*I*n the meantime, though, the stories about the goings-on at Cleopatra's fabulous court in Alexandria had spread around the army barracks in Rome. The soldiers were keen to hear more.

"We've heard all about your Egyptian feasts," one of them said to Enobarbus. "Is it true that you roast *eight* wild boar just for breakfast? And what about this famous Cleopatra – is she really as enchanting as they say?"

"Even more so," admitted Enobarbus. Gruff old soldier that he was, even he had been impressed by Cleopatra. He began to tell the soldiers about the day when he and Antony had first caught sight of her...

"We were by the river, and she arrived in her royal barge. All gold, it was – in the sunlight it almost seemed to burn on the water. You've never seen anything like it. The sails were all silk, and they were perfumed – the scent made your head spin. There were dozens of servants, some rowing, some waving fans to keep her cool. And then we saw her, Cleopatra, dressed in golden robes just like a goddess – like Venus herself!

Antony didn't stand a chance. Fell for her right away, he did, and I don't blame him. She is the most bewitching woman I have ever met. You would never grow tired of a woman like that," sighed Enobarbus.

The soldiers listened, wide-eyed. "But now he must give her up!" they said.

"Never!" said Enobarbus. Antony will *never* be able to tear himself away from her. You mark my words, this marriage to Octavia will be more trouble than it's worth."

Back in Egypt, Cleopatra heard the news of Antony's marriage and flew into a jealous rage. She was so angry she almost killed the poor messenger who'd come from Rome.

"I'll have you whipped with wire, and stewed in brine!" she shrieked, beating him and dragging him about the palace by his hair.

"Your majesty!" begged the poor man. "It's not my fault, I only brought the message. Let me go!"

But Cleopatra was beside herself. She threatened him with more and more horrible punishments. Eventually she calmed down just long enough to send him back to Rome to bring her a proper report on Antony's new wife.

A few weeks later the messenger was back in Alexandria. This time, however, he was clever enough to tell the queen what she wanted to hear.

"Hah! Short, round-faced and mousy, you say?" smiled Cleopatra. "Perfect. Antony will soon be bored with her and will come back to me!"

Although they had been prepared to go to war, Octavius and Antony managed to make peace with Pompey. To celebrate, Pompey held a feast on one of his ships. Everybody got drunk, especially Lepidus, who had to be carried off the ship!

"This is almost as good as an Alexandrian feast!" roared Pompey in delight.

But Octavius hardly drank anything and left the party early.

It seemed that the danger was over, and Antony was sent to Athens with his new wife. But when they arrived the news came that Octavius had attacked Pompey after all.

"And not only that," stormed Antony, "but he spoke scornfully of me in public! If you want your brother and me to remain friends, Octavia, you'd better go back to Rome and talk to him..."

But that wasn't all. Having used Lepidus as an ally in the war, Octavius now wanted him out of the way.

"He found some old letters Lepidus had once written to Pompey," one of the soldiers told Enobarbus. "He's accused Lepidus of being a traitor and had him thrown in jail."

Octavius was rid of one of his rivals. Now there was only Antony to deal with.

Soon, Octavius had news that almost made him explode with rage. Antony was back in Egypt with Cleopatra. "And if that weren't enough," he fumed, "they've crowned themselves king and queen of all the Eastern world. They sat on golden thrones in the public square. And I hear that Cleopatra had the nerve to dress up as the goddess, Isis! How dare they!"

It was a great insult to Rome. Worse still,
Octavius feared that Antony might be planning
his own rebellion against the Empire. But the
final straw for Octavius was the news that
Antony had deserted Octavia, his beloved
sister. He declared war on Egypt.

The Roman and Egyptian armies met for a great sea battle at a place called Actium.

"But why are we fighting at sea?" asked Enobarbus and the other captains. "It's crazy. We're far more powerful on land. Octavius' ships are better and faster than ours – he'll have a great advantage. Why insist on fighting at sea?"

"Because he's challenged me to," said Antony, stubbornly. "No arguments. We fight at sea."

"And I'm coming, too," said Cleopatra firmly.

"But, madam," pleaded Enobarbus, "that's not a good idea. You'll only distract Antony when he should be concentrating on the battle. Please stay behind and watch from the shore."

"Don't tell me what to do!" she raged. "How dare you argue with me? I'm the queen of this country and I'm coming!"

And so the battle began. Although Octavius'
ships were better, Antony's soldiers fought
bravely. They even seemed to be winning. But
suddenly, Cleopatra's ship turned and sailed
away from the fighting.

As those on shore watched in horror,
Antony's ship followed hers.

"Like a cow stung by a wasp, she just took off – and he followed her! I can't believe it. I've never seen anything so shameful," cried one of the sailors.

"I know," sighed Enobarbus, covering his eyes. "I couldn't bear to watch."

The battle was lost.

Antony was so ashamed at what he had done that he could hardly face his soldiers.

"I've let you all down," he told them. "I'm no longer fit to be your leader. My treasure ship is in the harbour, full of gold. Take it all and leave me. Go and find yourselves a better general to follow."

Cleopatra tried to console Anthony but he was in the depths of despair.

"Now I'll have to go crawling to that pompous young Octavius, begging for mercy," he said. "I'll resign from the army and see if he'll let me live out my life here in Egypt as just an ordinary citizen. He'll grant me that, at least."

*B*ut Octavius would have none of it. He wanted Antony to be his prisoner once and for all. He offered to make a secret treaty with Cleopatra.

When Antony heard this he was furious, and his anger made him brave again. "Come on, men," he shouted in a rousing speech. "Tomorrow we'll take on that cocky young Octavius again, and this time we can beat him. We'll show him what Egyptians are made of!"

But this time no one really believed that Antony could win. The night before the battle, there was a feeling of doom in the air. The soldiers heard strange noises and the sound of music in the dark, and they began to be afraid.

"It looks like our general's luck has finally run out," they muttered to each other as they waited in their tents.

Even the faithful Enobarbus finally had to admit that his old friend had gone too far. "Now Antony's really lost his head," he told himself. "It's madness – this time he's done for. I'd better start looking out for myself. Best to go over to Octavius now, before it's too late."

Enobarbus was right. In the battle the following morning, just at the crucial moment, Cleopatra's soldiers let Antony down again. Suddenly, they put down their weapons and surrendered to Octavius.

It was all over, and this time Antony knew it.

He was almost out of his mind with fury. In his madness he blamed Cleopatra for everything. "She has betrayed me to that boy, Octavius," he raged. "How could she have done this to me? I'll take my revenge on her, and then all that's left is to kill myself!"

For once Cleopatra was afraid of Antony. She ran away and shut herself up in the palace with her ladies-in-waiting.

Then she had an idea. "Go to Antony and tell him I've killed myself," she commanded a servant. "Tell him my last words were 'Antony, Antony'. Make it sound really tragic – and then come back and tell me how he takes it!"

That should do it, she thought to herself. When he hears that he'll be sorry. And then when he finds I'm *not* dead, he'll be so pleased that I'll be able to talk him round as usual.

But Cleopatra's plan went sadly wrong. When Antony heard that Cleopatra was dead, he no longer wanted to live.

"There's nothing left for me now," he said wearily, taking off his armour and picking up his sword. "I'll join you in death, Cleopatra," he said, as he pointed the sword at his heart. "Wait for me, my love—"

By the time his soldiers arrived, Antony was badly wounded but still alive. They carried him to the palace where Cleopatra was hiding. She wept when she realized what she had done, but it was too late.

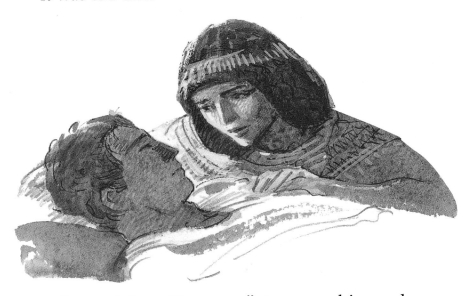

"I am dying, Cleopatra," Antony whispered. "I'm sorry for everything. Try to remember me as I used to be, not like this. And remember, when I am dead, do not trust Octavius. Now, give me one last kiss—" And with that he was dead.

Left alone, all Cleopatra could do was wait for Octavius to arrive and take her prisoner. She knew that she would be taken in triumph to Rome, where the crowds would make fun of her.

"I know what those Romans are like," she thought. "They make up plays about things like this. They'll put on a silly pantomime, and they'll have some drippy boy actor with a squeaky voice dressed up as me – Queen of Egypt! No, I can't bear it!"

Cleopatra had one final plan.

She sent for a fruit-seller to bring her a basket
of figs. When the basket arrived, there was a
poisonous snake hidden in it. She called her
ladies-in-waiting and commanded them to dress
her up in all her finery, her royal robes and her
crown. Then, carefully, she took the snake out
of the basket and placed it on her skin.

The snake's bite was swift and the poison was deadly. As it took effect Cleopatra cried, "Thank you, snake, for being so gentle. Antony, I'm coming to you – there's no reason to stay here any longer."

When Octavius and his men arrived, they found Cleopatra and her ladies-in-waiting all lying dead.

"Brave right to the last," he said, a little sadly. "In the end she found her own way to escape me. She was indeed a true and noble queen. She and Antony must be buried together and I will give them a magnificent funeral. No grave on earth will have in it a more famous couple."

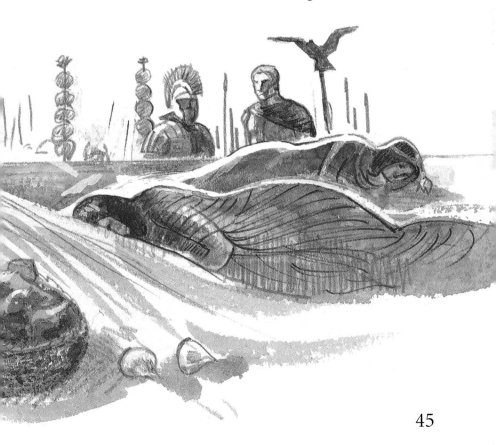

Then young Octavius set out for Rome. All his enemies were gone. Now he alone ruled the great Roman Empire.